The Sea
Monster

For Dom, Tom and Andy

THE SEA MONSTER
A JONATHAN CAPE BOOK 0 224 07025 8

Published in Great Britain by Jonathan Cape, an imprint of Random House Children's Books

This edition published 2005

1 3 5 7 9 10 8 6 4 2

Copyright © Chris Wormell, 2005

The right of Chris Wormell to be identified as the author of this work has been asserted in accordance with the Copyright, Designs and Patents Act 1988.

RANDOM HOUSE CHILDREN'S BOOKS 61-63 Uxbridge Road, London W5 5SA A division of The Random House Group Ltd

RANDOM HOUSE AUSTRALIA (PTY) LTD 20 Alfred Street, Milsons Point, Sydney, New South Wales 2061, Australia

RANDOM HOUSE NEW ZEALAND LTD 18 Poland Road, Glenfield, Auckland 10, New Zealand

RANDOM HOUSE (PTY) LTD Endulini, 5A Jubilee Road, Parktown 2193, South Africa

THE RANDOM HOUSE GROUP Limited Reg. No. 954009
www.**kids**at**randomhouse**.co.uk

A CIP catalogue record for this book is available from the British Library.

Printed in China

The Sea Monster

CHRIS WORMELL

A TOM MASCHLER BOOK
JONATHAN CAPE · LONDON

Down at the bottom of the ocean
there lived a great sea monster.
Barnacles and limpets clung to his scaly skin
and seaweed grew from every wrinkle.
In the gloom his eyes shone bright green.
Most of the time he stayed down in
the wavering kelp, watching the boats sail by.

But sometimes, early in the morning, he would swim up to the shore and sit among the rocks at the corner of a lonely beach.

He would sit very still,
and the seaweed hid his bright eyes
so no one ever saw him there.
Mostly he was content just to watch.

One day a boy came
down to the beach with
his dog, to sail a little
boat in the tide pools.

Among the rocks at the corner
of the beach he found a deep pool
where the water was crystal clear.
As he watched sea anemones and crabs
at the bottom, the boy had the
feeling *he* was being watched.

Then he saw something
shining bright green, high up
on a seaweed-covered rock,
and he started to climb.
His dog began to bark.

"My boat!" cried the boy,
as the sea took his little yacht
and carried it out among the
waves. He scrambled down
but it was too late; the boat
was far out of reach.

The boy dived in,
but the ocean current
had caught the boat
and was taking
it further out to sea.

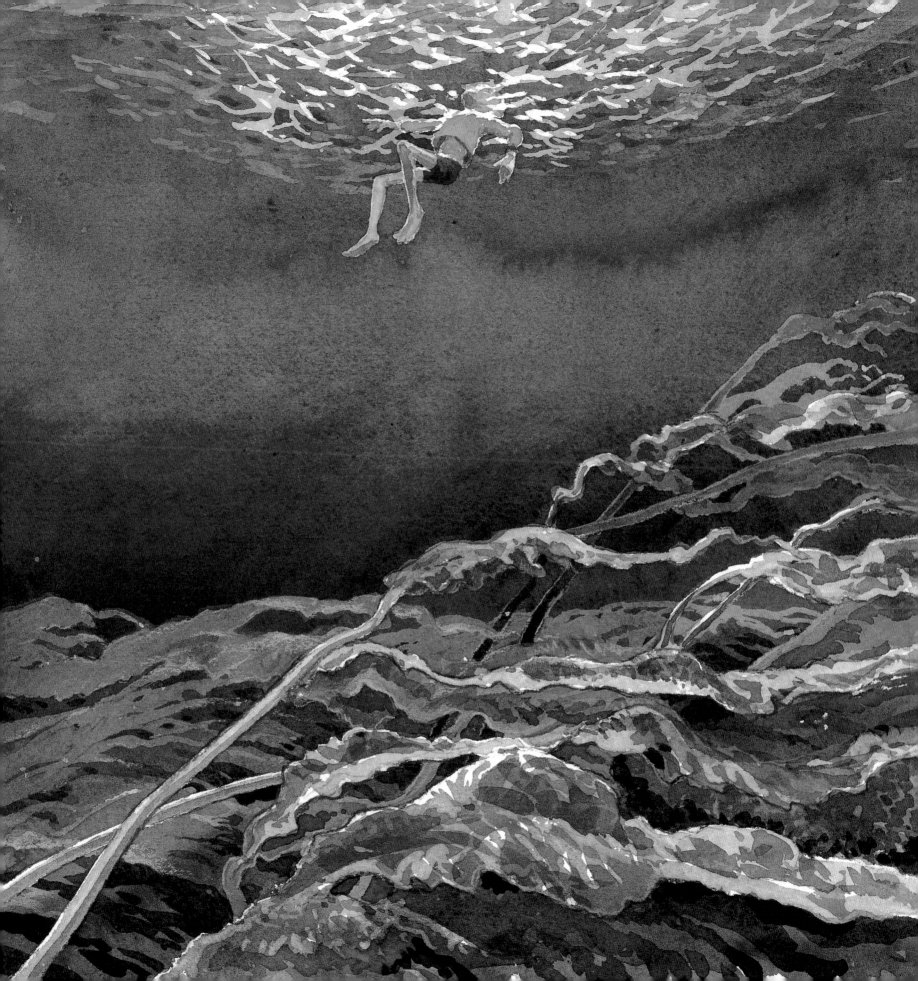

The current caught the boy too, and soon he was far out in the deep water beyond the bay. He could just hear the barking of his dog, echoing among the rocks.

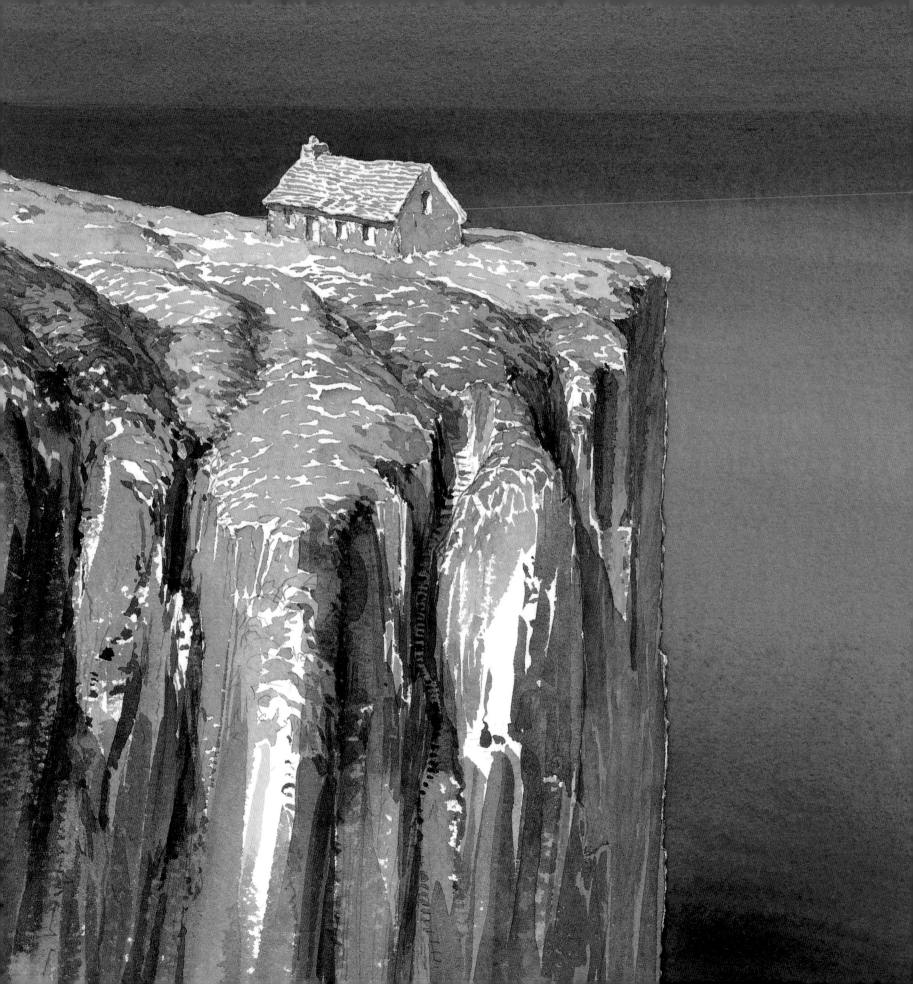

High on the cliff above the corner of the beach,
in a grey stone cottage, there lived an old fisherman.
It was a while since he had sailed the seas
catching fish and most of the time now
he made model boats . . .

. . . or sat alone
on the cliff top
watching the
boats sail by.
He saw seals
and porpoises
and great basking sharks, and sometimes he saw
strange green lights shining in the murky deep.
On this morning he heard barking in the bay below
and, looking down, saw a little white dog jumping
from rock to rock and splashing in the surf.
Turning to the ocean, the old fisherman could just
make out the head of a boy among the distant waves.

Beside the cottage, stone steps climbed down the cliff. It was a long time since the old fisherman had been that way, but he could still run down, two steps at a time.

At the bottom he kept a boat hidden among the rocks.

Although it was years since he'd rowed the boat,
the fisherman could still pull through the waves
like in the old days.

Far out into the ocean the old fisherman rowed,
but he saw no sign of the boy. The waves grew
big and the sky grew dark and the old man
had almost given up hope, when suddenly
the little white dog began
to bark.

And there, on a round rock covered
with barnacles and limpets, and with
seaweed growing from every crack,
they found the boy.

Later, safely back at the old fisherman's cottage,
the boy looked out over the vast ocean.
"That's strange," he said. "It's low tide, isn't it?
And yet there's no sign of that rock where you found me."

The old fisherman smiled. "Some rocks *are* strange,"
he said. "They pop up just when you need them
and then you never see them again."
The boy thought about this.
"And after all that I still lost my boat," he said.
"Never mind, you shall have this one,"
declared the old fisherman, presenting the boy
with a model boat he had just finished making.

Down at the bottom of the ocean,
among the wavering kelp,
the great sea monster sat.
And in his hand he held a little toy boat . . .